WELCOME TO

Beast Quest

Collect the special coins in this book.
You will earn one gold coin for
every chapter you read.

Once you have finished all the chapters,
find out what to do with your gold coins at
the back of the book.

With special thanks to Tabitha Jones

For Maya Piotrowicz

www.beastquest.co.uk

ORCHARD BOOKS

First published in Great Britain in 2021 by The Watts Publishing Group

1 3 5 7 9 10 8 6 4 2

Text © 2021 Beast Quest Limited
Cover and inside illustrations by Steve Sims
© Beast Quest Limited 2021

Beast Quest is a registered trademark of Beast Quest Limited
Series created by Beast Quest Limited, London

A CIP catalogue record for this book is available from the British Library.

ISBN 978 1 40836 222 8

Printed in Great Britain

The paper and board used in this book are made from wood from responsible sources

Orchard Books
An imprint of Hachette Children's Group
Part of The Watts Publishing Group Limited
Carmelite House, 50 Victoria Embankment, London EC4Y 0DZ

An Hachette UK Company
www.hachette.co.uk
www.hachettechildrens.co.uk

BixarA
THE HORNED DRAGON

BY ADAM BLADE

ORCHARD

CONTENTS

STORY ONE

THE DRAGON KING

Dear King Hugo,

I write to you as a loyal subject with a grave concern. I am the Chieftain of Merival. I am sure Your Majesty is aware that we are a small, unassuming harbour town. We have no quarrel with anybody...

But now, sire, we find ourselves under constant attack from our island neighbours, the villains of Thalassi. Daily, they harass our fishermen, and launch merciless raids on our defenceless villages. They think that they can do so without consequence, because they believe Avantia no longer cares for its distant, north-easterly regions.

I beg Your Majesty, prove them wrong! Please, send help at once!

Rutger

Chieftain of Merival

A DIPLOMATIC MISSION

A thin crescent moon hung in the twilit sky above the rocky heathland. Elenna's muscles ached from riding all day with Tom, Daltec, Captain Harkman and King Hugo. Even her chestnut mare's steady trot had begun to flag. They were heading to Merival, a small harbour town in the far north of Hugo's kingdom. The town had been repeatedly plundered by warriors from the neighbouring island of Thalassi, and Hugo intended to restore peace – by diplomatic means, if possible. Elenna straightened her back, unkinking her tired muscles, and took a deep breath of the cool evening air. Her heart lifted as she caught the first salty tang of seaweed on the breeze.

"I can smell the sea," she told the others. "We must be almost there."

"Not far to go now," Captain Harkman said. His burly warhorse pricked its ears and quickened its step, as if it understood, but Harkman's expression was grim as he gazed towards the horizon. "I just wish we knew what we are likely to find when we reach Thalassi."

"Something to eat, if we're lucky," Tom said. He was riding at Elenna's side on Storm, his black stallion. "I've heard that Thalassians are well known for their feasting. I hope those rumours are true!"

Elenna laughed. "You're always hungry." But actually, her own stomach growled. They had left Hugo's palace before dawn, and had ridden all day with only short breaks to water their horses.

"I'm afraid the Thalassians are as famous for their fighting as they are for feasting," King Hugo said. "We're just as likely to be greeted with swords as we are with food. In recent years, it seems they have become decidedly unfriendly towards visitors."

"Secretive, too," Daltec said. "I couldn't even find out who their current ruler is." The young wizard had passed much of his time on the journey perfecting his magical juggling tricks. Four apples now spun in the air before him.

"You do know that using magic to juggle is cheating!" Captain Harkman said. He shot out a hand, snatching one of the fruits, then sank his teeth into it with a crunch.

"Hey!" Daltec said. "I was saving that!"

"It's quite possible," Hugo said, "those apples will be our only dinner tonight. How I would love a hot meal and a long bath back at the palace!"

"Which is where you should be," Tom said. "It would have been far safer to let us investigate without you."

"Nonsense!" Hugo snorted. "It's been too long since I travelled to this part of my kingdom, and it's my duty to resolve any conflict. Also, I'm intrigued.

My father used to speak quite highly of the old ruler, King Hafor. He was once known as the Dragon King, and was said to rule with a magnificent Beast at his side."

Elenna inhaled sharply. She noticed Tom's body tense too.

"This is the first I've heard of Beasts," Tom said. "I thought this mission was supposed to be diplomatic. If you'd spoken of a dragon before, I would have strongly advised you to stay at home, sire!"

Hugo smiled and shrugged. "It was long ago," he said. "If there was a dragon on the island of Thalassi now, I think we'd know of it."

They had reached a craggy plateau. The rough heathland

dropped away ahead, revealing a horseshoe of rocky coastline cradling an inky stretch of sea. The hunched shapes of buildings hugged the shore, but with only a few scattered lights visible, the dwellings looked dark and uninviting.

As they drew closer to the harbour town, Elenna noticed that several of the buildings were little more than skeletons, the tips of blackened timbers jutting up like broken bones. Her skin prickled with dread. Ships bobbed in the harbour, but many of these, too, were charred shells with tattered sails.

"Things look worse than I had feared," Harkman muttered.

Elenna's worry deepened as they

rode on through fields empty of livestock, and across plots of charred stubble that must once have been crops. She spotted a burned-out barn, then a farmhouse with dark windows. Apart from the occasional bark of a dog, the place was eerily quiet.

They soon reached the outskirts of the harbour town. A muscular figure with shaggy hair and beard stepped from the doorway of a watchtower. Elenna reached for her bow, but the man raised a hand in greeting, and she let her weapon be.

Hugo pulled his horse to a stop. As she followed suit, Elenna saw the man was middle-aged with the tanned, lined skin of a fisherman. But his broad frame was stooped, and his

eyes hollow and weary beneath their thick dark brows. He bowed before Hugo.

"Thank you for coming, Your Majesty," the man said. "I am Rutger. Welcome to Merival…" His lips twisted into a wry smile. "Or what is left of it, anyway."

Hugo frowned as he took in the still smoking remains of a nearby house.

"The Thalassians did all this?" he asked.

Rutger nodded. "They used to keep to themselves, but now barely a week goes by without a raid. They rule the sea, too. I am one of the few left who will venture on to the water. I am afraid we can't offer you the hospitality we would like, but we have soup and ale, and can give you a warm bed for the night."

Hugo shook his head. "No, we won't take what little you have. And I mean to get the bottom of this at once. Please, escort us to Thalassi."

"Very well," Rutger said. He led them through dim, deserted streets and down to the harbour, where the burned hulls of vessels littered a narrow shingle beach.

By the time their horses were fed, and they had all climbed aboard Rutger's rowing boat, the sky was almost completely dark. A pale, cold mist rose from the water.

Elenna strained her eyes to see through the swirling whiteness as Rutger rowed with strong, steady strokes. Silence enveloped them. Even the slap of the water against the hull was muffled. At Elenna's side, Tom sat tense and alert, his hand on the hilt of his sword. Eventually, through a break in the mist, she caught a glimpse of high, dark cliffs, as jagged as broken teeth.

Thalassi...

"I don't know how much closer I can take you without fear of running aground," Rutger said.

"Let me help," Daltec replied. He muttered a short incantation, then waved a hand. The fog billowed away, revealing a clear stretch of calm, black water.

And something else! A huge dark shape reared towards them through

the mist. Elenna snatched her bow
from her back, heart hammering. *A
longship!* And it was right on top of
them!

HAFOR'S HALL

"Stop where you are!" a curt female voice barked. A sudden flare of torchlight on board the longship revealed a small woman dressed in studded leather, glaring down at them from the prow. Behind her, broad-shouldered warriors with round shields and longswords manned the boat.

Tom drew his sword and Elenna

fitted an arrow to her bow.

"Put down your weapons and turn back!" the woman shouted. She was slender, and no taller than Elenna, but her eyes were fierce. She brandished her torch like a club.

"I am King Hugo of Avantia!" Hugo replied. "This is my kingdom. Let us pass!"

"I don't care who you are!" the woman called back. "I am Venga, daughter of Chief Hafor. If you come any closer, I will set your boat alight!" She thrust her flaming torch towards them.

I don't think so… Elenna let her arrow fly. It hit the torch with a satisfying thud, knocking it from the woman's grip and into the fjord.

Furious roars erupted from the men on the longship. Many leapt to their feet, waving swords and axes. Venga drew her own blade from a scabbard at her hip.

"Turn back, or die!" she cried.

"I am your king," Hugo said calmly. "And I come in peace. Unless you want me to return with the full Avantian fleet, you *will* take me to your commander."

The woman's eyes narrowed and she hitched her chin. "If you come in peace, why do you carry weapons?" she demanded.

"We are ambassadors, not fools," King Hugo said. "However, if it will reassure you, we shall surrender our weapons."

"No..." Harkman said. "Your Majesty, I must insist that—"

"Captain!" the king said, cutting Harkman off. Then he turned back to the woman. "Do you accept my offer? Or shall I return with enough ships to storm your island?"

Venga frowned. "If you leave your weapons behind, you may come. Just you and one bodyguard."

"Your Majesty—" Harkman tried again but Hugo put up a hand to silence him. Elenna thought she could see a devious light in the king's eyes. He squared his shoulders and smoothed down his cloak, turning back to Venga.

"I will need my personal serving boy, too," Hugo said, gesturing to Tom. "I never go anywhere without him." Venga glanced at Tom and shrugged, clearly seeing no threat.

"Very well," she said. "The boy may accompany you."

"And me!" Elenna said. "I also serve

the king, and refuse to leave his side."

"No!" Venga's sharp eyes snapped towards Elenna. "Not the girl. I saw the way she wielded her bow. She is clearly no ordinary servant. She stays behind."

Elenna opened her mouth to protest, but Daltec put a hand on her shoulder. "Let them go," he murmured. "I have a plan."

"I accept your terms," Hugo said, taking his sword from his belt and laying it in the rowing boat. Captain Harkman grumbled, but did the same. Tom laid down his own sword and shield. Elenna noticed that he did not take off his magical belt.

Venga unfurled a rope ladder over the side of her ship and stepped back, waiting for them to board.

Captain Harkman went first, then Hugo. As Tom rose to follow, Elenna saw Daltec grip his arm.

"Take this," the wizard whispered, slipping a small ruby ring on to Tom's finger. Tom looked puzzled, but with Venga glaring down at them, there was no time for questions. He climbed the ladder, joining Harkman and Hugo on the deck of the longship. Seeing her friends surrounded by so many armed warriors, Elenna had to fight the urge to follow them.

Tom's no defenceless child, she reminded herself. *He'll know what to do...*

Venga hauled up her ladder then barked a command. The crew of the longship began to row, turning the vessel towards the rocky island, still shrouded in mist.

"Let's go," Daltec told Rutger. The man took up his oars and started back towards the harbour.

"What was the ring for?" Elenna asked Daltec, once they were out of earshot of Venga's ship.

"It's a new form of magic I've been working on," Daltec said. He lifted his hand, and Elenna saw he was wearing a ring too. "It will give me a bird's eye view of wherever Tom goes. Watch." Daltec's ring glowed brightly for a moment, like an ember, and a thin trail of red smoke emerged, quickly thickening to a cloud that hung in the air just above the ruby.

Daltec blew on to the smoke. The centre cleared, and Elenna gasped. She could see the ship that had just left them, rowing though the mist towards the craggy island ahead. The vision was lit by a strange red glow so that Elenna could clearly make out Tom and the others on board. They were standing side by side near the bow of the ship, gazing towards Thalassi. Beyond them, Elenna could see a great natural archway of rock set in the cliff-face. The longship slipped through it and out into a high-sided fjord, its water as smooth and dark as volcanic glass. The ship followed the fjord swiftly inland, soon nearing the far shore. Looking down from her bird's

eye view, Elenna made out a rocky
harbour at the end of the waterway.
Overlooking the harbour was a
square fortress surrounded by high

wooden ramparts and watchtowers.

"Welcome to Hafor's Hall," Venga said. Her voice reached Elenna clearly enough, but sounded as thin and distorted as if it were carried by the wind. Elenna saw Hugo's brows shoot up in surprise.

"I... How is Hafor these days?" he asked. "I thought he might have passed his crown on by now?"

Venga's face flushed and she turned away, hiding it from the king. "My father is still in very good health, thank you," she said.

The longship drew up beside a wooden jetty. Several burly men dressed in furs and leathers hurried from Hafor's Hall to help it dock. Elenna looked more closely at the fortress. It had narrow windows, and no ornamentation. Not even a flag. Suspended walkways joined the towers and outbuildings of the main fort, and watch fires burned along the ramparts. Their flames glinted off massive catapults and crossbows, all pointed towards the sky.

Elenna saw Tom's brow crease into a puzzled frown as he looked up at the ranks of weaponry; far more than could be needed to face any threat from Merival. She knew he was thinking the same as her. *What are the Thalassians so afraid of?*

1

A MEAGRE FEAST

The contented sound of the horses munching the oats in their nosebags mingled with the hush of gentle waves, but Elenna sat tense and alert, staring into the churning fog. As soon as Rutger had brought them ashore, she and Daltec had settled the animals, then found a smooth boulder overlooking the harbour. Daltec pulled his cloak closer about him, against the chill of the night. Elenna bit her lip. *I wish I was at Tom's side!*

Resting his hand on the stone between them, Daltec muttered an incantation. Elenna watched a tendril of smoke snake from the ruby.

Once a cloud had gathered above Daltec's ring, he blew into it once more, and just as before, a picture emerged, illuminated by a halo of red light.

Elenna made out Tom first, striding forwards at King Hugo's side with Captain Harkman. Venga marched ahead of them, flanked by two huge guards each carrying massive double-headed axes. The big men dwarfed Venga, but with her quick step and straight bearing, she looked every bit the warrior they did. Her long, fair hair was gathered into a thick braid that reached almost to her waist. At her belt, she wore a longsword and an axe, as well as several wicked-looking knives. Elenna could see the pommels of more knives sticking out from the woman's fur boots. *She looks ready for anything – but why?*

Elenna glanced at Tom's sword and shield, lying beside her, and let out an uneasy sigh. Watching her friends walking into danger, unarmed... It was almost too much to bear.

She turned her attention back to the glowing image. Venga had stopped before a pair of heavy wooden doors.

"Take me to Hafor at once," Hugo demanded.

Venga shook her head. "You are our

guests now. First you must rest, then we shall feast!"

The wooden doors swung inwards, and Venga marched through with her guards. Hugo and the others followed. Elenna felt a moment's worry that she would lose sight of her friends, but the vision dipped after them, showing a dimly lit antechamber with a smoking fire in a central hearth. Squat timber doorways led to corridors on each side, and a wide staircase climbed to a pair of larger double doors ahead.

Venga turned. "My guards will show you to your rooms. I will announce your arrival to my father." She left at once, heading up the staircase. One of the guards – a sandy-haired, bearded man with a crooked nose –

led Tom, Harkman and King Hugo down a dingy corridor lit with smoking torches. He stopped at a door and gestured inside. Hugo went first, followed by Harkman. Through the door, Elenna could see a large chamber with a massive bed, covered in furs. A fired burned in the grate, and a flagon of wine stood on a table beside a ewer of water and a washing bowl. Above the bed was a long, roughly woven tapestry, depicting a man wielding a two-headed axe, battling what looked like a dragon.

"What Beast is that?" Tom asked the guard.

The big man shrugged. "A dragon," he said. "Hafor defeated it, long ago."

"Amazing!" Tom said. "I've always

been fascinated by Beasts. What was it called?"

The man shrugged again. "As I said, it was long ago." The broad warrior lifted his gaze to the king, who had seated himself on the edge of the bed. "You will be summoned when our feast is ready," he said. Tom began to move towards the king, but the guard caught his shoulder roughly. "Not you!" he grunted. "You, follow me."

The guard led Tom further along the corridor, to a smaller doorway at the end. Elenna caught a movement in the shadows as Tom entered, and wrinkled her nose. *A rat!*

Tom glanced around the dark, cramped chamber and let out a sigh. A blanket lay on a straw mattress in one corner. There was a bucket in another. Elenna grimaced. Even the dungeons at Hugo's palace were more inviting than this.

Once the guard's footsteps had retreated, Tom sat heavily on the mattress. Elenna watched him gaze about, then frown, as if troubled by more than the cell's grimy walls.

Daltec bent low over his ring. "Tom," he said, his voice echoing strangely.

Tom's head snapped up, and he looked wide-eyed into the shadows. "Daltec?" he hissed. "Where are you?"

"In Merival," Daltec said. "I can see you and speak with you using the magic of the ruby ring I gave you to wear. Are you all right?"

Tom rubbed a hand over his face, and

shook his head. "There is something wrong here," he said. He gestured to the red jewel in the belt round his waist. "I can feel the presence of a Beast."

"Could it be the dragon in the tapestry?" Elenna asked.

"Possibly," Tom said. "But I don't know… I think it's in pain, or…a kind of anguish. I've never felt anything like—" A sudden harsh knock at the door cut Tom off. He leapt to his feet, just as Venga shoved the door open and thrust her head inside.

"Who were you talking to?" she snapped.

Tom hesitated, but only for a heartbeat. "I was thinking out loud," he said. "I've heard great things about the feasts you hold here. I was wondering when supper would be."

Venga glared for a moment, but then nodded curtly. "If you are ready, follow me. I will take you to the feasting hall."

After collecting Hugo and Captain Harkman, Venga showed Tom and the others back the way they had come and up the staircase through the double doors. A wave of noise escaped the vast, high-ceilinged chamber, already packed with men and women seated at long tables. Skinny dogs lying at their masters' feet watched eagerly as servants poured mead into drinking horns and placed trenchers of black bread before the diners. Hugo and Harkman were led to a raised dais near the hearth and seated beside an empty throne. Before Tom could take his own seat, a bustling serving woman thrust a jug of mead into his hand. A flicker of irritation crossed Tom's face, but he stationed himself at Hugo's shoulder and poured for Harkman and the king.

Steaming cauldrons of soup were brought in next and set down on the

boards. Then, with still no sign of Hafor, Venga seated herself on the other side of the empty throne, and the feasting began.

Tom ladled out bowls of what looked like thin soup for the king and the captain, and they each tore chunks from their bread. Elenna saw Harkman mutter something to King Hugo, who glanced around, then nodded. The captain's face was flushed, and he leered as if he'd had too much mead, but Elenna had seen him play this part before. If he acted a fool, it was more likely someone would let important information slip.

"When is the meat coming?" Harkman asked a muscular woman with tattooed arms, seated beside him. "I heard that Thalassi had ten thousand sheep and goats. Why are we dining on fish broth?"

The woman glared coldly back at him. Men at nearby tables turned to stare at the stranger, their raucous conversation dying. But before the woman could answer, a sudden cheer went up as a young man, clad in a gold-studded leather jerkin and thick furs, strode into the room. A circlet of gold rested on his long, dark curls, and the hilt of his axe glittered with jewels. He was clearly King Hafor – but from his bulging muscles and smooth, tanned skin, Elenna would have said he was younger than Venga.

"All hail King Hafor!" Venga shouted, raising her horn. King Hugo and

Harkman exchanged bewildered glances, but joined the toast, giving cheers too as Hafor took his throne.

Once the noise had died down, King Hugo turned to the young man at his side.

"Hafor, I must speak to you regarding the recent raids on Merival," Hugo said.

Hafor turned with a good-humoured smile, his blue eyes bright and merry. "Let it wait until tomorrow! Tonight is for merriment!" Hafor drained his horn in one gulp, and held it up for Tom to refill. King Hugo did the same, and Elenna thought she saw him suppress a grimace at the taste of the liquor. For a while, everyone ate hungrily, and apart from a pair of dogs squabbling over a hunk of bread, the only sounds were slurping and chomping.

"Hafor," Harkman called, from his seat beside Hugo. "Maybe you can share with us the secret of your good health?" Hafor glanced up at him, still chewing, but with a sudden icy look in his eyes. "Come on!" Harkman went on. "If I had the good fortune to look younger than my daughter, I wouldn't keep the recipe to myself."

"That is no way to speak to our king!" the tattooed woman at Harkman's side snapped. "You know nothing of our ways!"

Harkman nodded. "That is why I am asking," he said, too loudly. "I am sure everyone in Avantia would like to know the secret of eternal youth.

Surely Hafor must be four score, at least. Or older."

The woman slammed down her drinking horn. "How dare you question our king about his age?"

"But why not share his good fortune? I don't see the harm," Harkman replied. The woman drew back her fist and swiped a punch at him. Elenna winced, but before the blow could land, Tom grabbed the woman's wrist from behind and held it fast. She turned to him, open-mouthed with angry surprise.

"Stop this foolishness at once!" Hafor bellowed from his throne, a pained look crossing his smooth brow. Elenna noticed that it suddenly didn't look *quite* as smooth as before. In fact, she could see a streak of grey in his hair, and lines around his eyes and mouth. *They weren't there before...*

Hafor put a hand to his head. "All this noise and bickering displeases me. I will retire at once. Venga – bring wine to my chamber." Harkman and Hugo stared in confusion as Venga swept from the hall with Hafor hobbling at her side, half leaning on her arm. Tom's dark gaze was troubled as he watched them go.

Something very strange is going on, Elenna thought. *Tom feels it too.* Daltec muttered a few words and the vision faded, leaving just a cloud of red-tinged smoke.

"What was all that about?" Elenna asked. Daltec just sighed. He looked

exhausted, his face pale and pinched. Clearly, using his magic on top of riding all day had taken its toll.

"I don't know," he said. "But there is more to all of this than just a few raids. Hafor must have access to some magic I have never come across before —

magic that thwarts the ageing process."

Elenna thought of what Tom had said, about a Beast in distress. "We should head to the island," she said. "I think the others are in danger."

Daltec shook his head. "Let's wait — for now, at least. You saw how secretive they are. Tom and the king need time to find out what's going on. If we arrive on the island without permission, that will put an end to any peaceful talks. And we will be badly outnumbered. I think you are right, though. There is something evil going on. And we need to figure out if King Hafor is up to something…" Daltec's shoulders slumped. "But before we do anything else, I must rest."

HIDDEN SECRETS

Elenna and Daltec led the horses
after Rutger to a small, thatched
inn overlooking the harbour. Part of
the roof had been burned away and
replaced with boards, but a warm
light shone through the windows.
After helping to stable the horses,
Rutger left them, heading to his own
cottage near the shore. Elenna and
Daltec gathered Tom's sword and

shield, as well as the supplies they would need for the night, then headed inside.

A tired-looking young woman greeted them. She showed them to a simple room with a fire and two cots. After a meal of bread and cheese, Daltec stretched out on his mattress and wrapped his cloak around himself. Elenna curled up on her own bed and tried to sleep, but images of Hafor and his strange behaviour churned in her mind and kept her awake.

Finally, she decided to stop trying to rest, and sat up to see Daltec staring at the ceiling.

"Can we check on Tom and the others again?" Elenna asked him.

"I'm too worried to sleep, so we may as well," Daltec sighed, swinging his legs over the edge of his bed. Elenna took a seat next to him and waited while he conjured the magical red smoke from his ring.

This time, the mist cleared to show Tom lying on his lumpy straw tick, wide awake and chewing his lip.

"Tom?" Elenna said.

Tom's eyes widened. "Elenna?" he whispered into the darkness. "Are you watching?"

"Yes," she replied.

"I can feel the Beast again," Tom said. "And I'm worried. It seems so... *sad*. I'm going to take a look around, while everyone's asleep. I'll feel better, knowing that you're there."

"Be careful," Elenna whispered, watching Tom slip from the room and tiptoe along the dim corridor. She leaned close to Daltec's ring, listening for any sound, but it seemed the whole fortress was sleeping. She watched Tom creep back towards the banqueting hall, stepping almost silently past each closed door. When he neared the main antechamber, Elenna spotted a pair of guards exiting the feasting room. *A night patrol!* "Tom!" she hissed. "Stop!"

Tom halted, right at the end of the corridor. The two guards clomped down the staircase and swept their gazes across the entrance chamber, then took the passage to their right. Elenna let out a quivering breath. "All

clear," she told Tom. He ducked out
from his corridor, hurried through
the antechamber and slipped into the
hall.

Inside, the fire had burned low.
Several of the warriors from dinner
were now slumped in their seats,
snoring. Mead had spilled from the
horns. A dog under the table glanced
up at Tom, then sleepily settled its
muzzle back on its paws.

A floorboard creaked hollowly.
Elenna scanned the red-tinged vision,
and from her strange vantage point
she saw a hunched, ancient-looking
figure stooped in the doorway. "Hide!"
she gasped. Tom swiftly ducked
under a nearby table, just as the
old man entered the room. He was

dressed in warm furs over a long
white nightshirt. Wisps of snowy
hair showed from under his nightcap
and he gripped a walking stick in
one clawed, trembling hand as he
shuffled across the hall. Tom peered

from beneath the table as the old man made his slow way towards a long tapestry behind the dais at the rear wall. There, he fumbled with a bunch of keys before twitching the tapestry aside, revealing a door. After casting a furtive glance behind him, the man unlocked the door, sending a slender beam of cool blue light out into the hall. Then, soundlessly, he stepped through, letting the tapestry fall behind him.

A moment later, Tom emerged from beneath the table, crossed to the hanging and lifted the edge. Daltec muttered something, and Elenna's perspective shifted. Suddenly, it was as if she were seeing right *through* Tom's eyes, peering behind the tapestry into the strange, blue light. The hidden door opened directly on to a tiny room, no bigger than a cupboard. Inside was a high table bearing a velvet cushion, on which rested a huge egg that shone with a pale blue gleam – like the moon on a clear winter night. The old man reached out a shaking hand and laid it flat on the glowing shell. He gasped, then gave a long, satisfied sigh. Straightening his back, he lifted his head. *Black* curls flowed from beneath his cap over his shoulders, and his muscles seemed to swell.

Daltec draw in a sharp hiss of breath. "Hafor!" he murmured. Elenna recognised the young man from earlier, standing where the old man had been.

"The egg is somehow making him young again," she said, watching the wrinkles on the old man's hands vanish, leaving smooth tanned skin. Suddenly, she heard a footstep, close behind her. No – behind *Tom*.

"Trespasser!" cried a woman's voice. The vision jerked and reeled as Tom turned around to look at Venga, her sword straight out before her, and her eyes blazing with fury.

"This is treachery!" Hafor's voice roared. Elenna's vision reeled again, as Tom glanced over his shoulder to see Hafor raising his cane.

"*You* are the one in the wrong," Tom said. "That egg belongs to a Beast. You have stolen it!"

Hafor's face contorted with hate. His cane whipped out with a loud *crack* that made Elenna gasp, just before the vision went completely blank.

A FIELD OF BONES

Elenna leapt to her feet. "We have to help him!"

With a nod, Daltec rose. They made their way out into the night to find the fog had lifted and a brisk wind had risen, sending small, tattered clouds scudding across the starry sky. Elenna and Daltec hurried to Rutger's seafront cottage, then hammered on the door. After a pause, they hammered again. There was a bump and a curse, then Rutger answered, rubbing his eyes.

"What's going on?" he asked gruffly; but then, as he took in Elenna and Daltec's worried expressions, his tone

softened. "How can I help?"

"We need to borrow your boat," Elenna blurted. "Daltec's magic has shown us that Tom is in great danger."

"I'll row you to Thalassi," Rutger said, grabbing his cloak from by the door.

Daltec shook his head. "We need to you to stay here and get word to Queen Aroha if we don't return."

After a brief hesitation, Rutger nodded. "Take my rowing boat, and luck be with you. If you're not back by noon tomorrow, I'll send a search party and ask for back-up from the palace."

"Thank you," Elenna said, then took off, running towards the beach and finding Rutger's boat tied to the jetty just as they'd left it. She leapt aboard and grabbed the oars. Daltec untied the boat, stepped in and pushed off.

Elenna rowed hard and fast against the high, rolling waves that slapped against the bow. Daltec bent over his ring, muttering words to summon a vision; but after each attempt, he shook his head, frustrated.

"Tom must still be unconscious," he said. Elenna redoubled her pace, driving the oars through the water with all her strength. Her arms soon burned and sweat and sea spray stung her eyes, but she blinked it away and forced herself to keep going.

"I've got him!" Daltec exclaimed suddenly. "He's in a cell, and they've taken his belt. Tom!" he called, his voice echoing hollowly. "Are you all right?" Elenna strained to hear her friend's reply over the waves.

"Yes," Tom said, and Elenna's heart lifted. "They're going to put me on trial. But they can't do much with King Hugo here to back me."

"Hold tight," Daltec told him. "We're on our way too."

They approached the towering cliffs of Thalassi, and Elenna made for the archway in the rock. But as she neared it, a huge longship sailed through.

"I need help!" Elenna cried. The ship blazed with torchlight, showing at least twenty warriors aboard. Elenna could make out their hawkish

grimaces as they stared into the night;
could see the gleam of their weapons,
like fallen stars floating above the
sea. At the prow of the ship, two
burly warriors manned a pair of giant
catapults, loaded with rocks.

"There they are!" a harsh voice
shouted. The burly men took aim,
and with a triumphant roar, let their
missiles fly.

Daltec lifted his hand, sending
out an arc of silver light. *A force-
field!* Elenna realised. The first rock
slammed into the glowing arc and
ricocheted off, plunging into the
waves with a mighty *splash*. Another
chunk of rock hit an instant later,
then another, each falling away and
sending up plumes of water. The

small boat rocked wildly, and Daltec,
holding on with only one hand, pitched
forwards. Elenna tried to steady the
vessel with her oars, but another giant
missile splashed down right beside

them, making the boat lurch.

Daltec toppled sideways, cracking his head on the edge of the boat. His force-field flickered, and failed.

"Look out!" Elenna screamed, reaching for his cloak and missing as the biggest rock yet plummeted towards them. With a splintering *crash*, it hit the boat, smashing the boards, causing the vessel to buck. Elenna gripped the side, watching helplessly as the young wizard tumbled overboard, into the sea.

With icy water gushing in all around her, Elenna dropped to her knees and leaned over the side of the boat, holding an oar out towards Daltec. Wide-eyed and spluttering, he grabbed for it – but at that moment, another rock slammed into the boat, driving a splintered shard of wood deep into Elenna's thigh. She gasped, closing her eyes and clenching her teeth against the pain.

When she opened her eyes again, Daltec was gone. All she could see were foaming waves.

"Daltec!" she shouted. Ahead, the men on the longship loaded more ammunition into their catapults. Now waist-deep in water, Elenna thought of abandoning the boat, but she knew from the searing pain in her leg that she wouldn't be able to swim.

I can't drown, she thought. *Tom needs me!*

With a bloodthirsty cheer, the men on the longship hurled more rocks.

One smashed into the boards right beside her, and the rowing boat pitched, waves crashing over her head, filling her mouth and nose. She couldn't see. Her leg burned as if it was on fire... Panic gripped hold of her and she cast about frantically in the water. *I'm going to die!*

Then, with a gentle *pop*, everything went suddenly still and silent. Elenna blinked the saltwater from her eyes to find herself lying on her back in long grass, looking up at the night sky.

"Are you all right?" Daltec panted from nearby. Elenna struggled up to her elbows and saw the young wizard leaning against a rock, soaked through, with blood seeping from a gash on his forehead. He swayed, as if

he might faint at any moment.

"I think so," she answered, but even
as she spoke, the terrible searing pain
in her leg surged back. "Thanks to
you. Where are we?"

"I'm not sure," Daltec said, blinking woozily as he gazed about. "On Thalassi, is the best I can say. My magic was all but spent when I cast that last spell...but at least we're not inside a rock, or similar."

Elenna nodded. "You saved our lives – and with any luck, the Thalassians will think we drowned. Which means they won't be expecting us..." She looked down at the huge splinter of wood jutting from her thigh. Peeling back the torn fabric of her leggings, she exposed a deep red wound. Her stomach heaved at the sight, but she held her breath and gritted her teeth as she drew out the splinter. It was almost as long as her hand. Blood welled up immediately.

"Here," Daltec said, handing Elenna Tom's shield. She took Epos's healing talon from its place and held it against the bleeding cut. The throbbing pain faded and Elenna sighed with relief as the cut closed over.

"Thank you!" Elenna said, handing Daltec the talon. He quickly healed the cut on his own head, then clicked the talon back into Tom's shield.

"Which way?" Elenna asked.

Daltec gazed up at the stars. "I think if we head west," he said, pointing, "it will take us back towards the fort."

They set off across the field, traipsing through long grass and weeds. Though Epos's talon had healed the wound on Elenna's leg, it had done nothing to ease her exhaustion, or the weary ache in every muscle. Nor could it protect her from the keen wind driving through her wet clothes, chilling her to the bone. Daltec was even worse off, stumbling as he walked, his head bowed as if too heavy to lift.

Elenna stopped. "Lean on me," she said. Daltec smiled gratefully, and put an arm across her shoulder. Elenna wrapped her own arm around his waist, and they both trudged into the darkness again.

Before they had gone much further, Elenna's foot jarred against something half hidden in a tangle of weeds. Daltec almost toppled, but

Elenna steadied him just in time. She bent to look more closely at what had stopped them, and reeled back at the sight of empty eye sockets staring blindly up at her.

It was the skeleton of a sheep, picked completely clean.

Straightening, Elenna cast her gaze over the rest of the field, a shudder running through her. There were pale bones everywhere, gleaming in the weak moonlight. Daltec frowned as he took in the devastation all around them.

"What could have killed all these sheep?" he wondered aloud.

"A Beast," Elenna guessed. "That means the others are in more danger than I thought. Let's hurry!"

They started off again, half jogging, half hobbling. The rocky terrain rose and fell, but apart from a few fearful-looking goats huddled in the shadow of a jagged outcrop of stone, they saw no sign of any living thing. Suddenly a high, urgent whistle reached them on the wind. Elenna looked for the source of the sound, and spotted the dark opening of a cave in a low cliff.

"Hurry!" an old, cracked voice called as a bent figure appeared at the cave mouth, beckoning frantically. "Get in here now! If you stay out there, you'll be killed!"

6

ON TRIAL

Keeping her bow strung ready in case of a trick, Elenna made her way towards the figure in the cave with Daltec at her side. The man who had called out gripped her arm as soon as she was in reach.

"Follow me!" he said, tugging her into the shelter. His cheeks were lined and hollow, and a patched tunic hung loose on his wasted frame. Even as

tired as she was, Elenna could see he'd
be no match for her in a fight – and his
eyes, though wide with worry, looked
kindly enough. She lowered her bow
and, with Daltec right behind her,
followed the man into the cave. There,
they found a woman huddled before
a fire. Two small children slept in
bundles at her side, while a few skinny
goats dozed in a corner. *The man must
be a goatherd*, Elenna assumed.

"What are you doing out at this
time?" the woman asked, rising to
greet them. "Everyone knows Bixara
attacks anything outside at night."

"Who is Bixara?" Elenna asked,
although from the dread stirring in
her gut she had a pretty good idea.
A Beast...

The man and woman gaped at her. "The dragon, of course!" the man said, in a quivering voice. "You must be strangers here."

Daltec nodded. "We have come to Thalassi with King Hugo from the mainland. We were not aware of a

Beast here, or we would have come prepared. Still, I am a wizard, and Elenna is a warrior. We will help you with Bixara."

The woman, who Elenna assumed was the goatherd's wife, ran a doubtful gaze over them. "Bixara has already killed almost all of the sheep and goats on the island," she said. "Not for food, either – just to make us suffer, as far as I can tell. She will attack anyone out after dark. But, if you mean what you say about helping us, you are more than welcome to rest here with us until morning."

"Thank you," Elenna said, though the thought of stopping, even for an instant, filled her with frustration and worry. *Still, I can't rescue Tom if*

I get killed by a dragon. "If we could share your shelter for a brief rest, we would be very grateful," she said.

Daltec and Elenna set their backs against the stone wall of the cave. The goatherd and his wife lay back down on their pallet of furs. Once their breathing had settled into the gentle rhythm of sleep, Elenna turned to the wizard.

"Do you have enough energy to check on Tom?" she asked.

"Just about," Daltec said. He lifted his hand and with a few whispered words, conjured the red-tinted smoke from his ring. When the smoke cleared, Elenna saw her best friend standing before Hafor's dais in the feasting hall, held between two broad-shouldered warriors who were rubbing their eyes groggily. Venga was seated at her father's side, looking as if she had never slept, while King Hugo and Captain Harkman, still wearing their nightshirts, stood near Tom, guarded by more tired-looking men.

"King Hugo," Hafor said sternly, "this boy is accused of treachery, trespass and spying. How dare you come here under the pretence of peace and use such underhanded tactics in my own home!"

Captain Harkman clenched his jaw, his face flushed with anger. Hugo shook his head, frowning. "Tom is a simple servant," Hugo said. "I am certain he meant no harm."

Hafor slammed his fist down on the table before him. "Don't play me for a fool!" he boomed, spittle flying from his lips. "I know why you've come here. You intend to steal my egg – a trophy that is rightfully mine!"

"Rightfully yours?" Tom cried, his eyes flashing with fury. "*You* stole the egg. From a Beast. Its magic keeps you young!"

"I won it fair and square in battle!" Hafor shouted back.

Tom narrowed his eyes, his colour rising. "I know what's going on," Tom said. "I am Master of the Beasts, and I can feel Bixara's rage and anguish through the power of the red jewel in my belt. I know why you have no cattle and have to raid Merival for food. And I know why you need so many weapons, pointing at the sky. Bixara wants her egg back. Like any parent, human or Beast, she'll do whatever she can to rescue her young. And you're afraid...*rightly* afraid."

"I've heard enough!" Hafor boomed. "I sentence you to death!"

With a furious roar, Captain Harkman lunged forwards, driving a fist towards one of the men holding Tom. But a warrior gripped Harkman's shoulders and though he tugged and struggled to free himself, the guard held him fast.

"Father!" Venga said. "You don't need to kill anyone. Just exile them. Send them away!"

"Listen to your daughter!" King

Hugo shouted. "This is madness! You can't kill my servant. I am your king."

Hafor tore at his hair, his eyes wild and his teeth bared. "I can't risk word

of the egg getting out!" he cried.
"Everyone will want it then. No – I
will have the boy killed. You and your
bodyguard will rot in my dungeons –
and no one will ever know about my
precious egg!"

"Then all the ships in my army will
come to our aid," Hugo told him. "You
can't hope to get away with this!"

"Pah!" Hafor said, grinning now
his mind was made up. "I will make
sure no word of your arrival here ever
gets back to the palace. Guards! Take
our prisoners to the dungeon. At first
light, we will deliver the boy to Skull
Rock. And there he will die!"

Elenna looked up from the red-
tinged vision, cold horror washing
through her. Daltec met her gaze.

"It's as the king says," Daltec said, looking as worried as Elenna felt. "Hafor's mad. If Hugo doesn't return to the palace, Aroha will lead the whole army in an attack on Thalassi."

Elenna nodded. She glanced at the grey light now visible through the cave mouth and swallowed hard. "Yes, the army will come," she said. "But not until after Tom is dead. We have to get to Skull Rock before sunrise!"

TOO LATE!

Elenna shook the goatherd awake.

"What is it?" he asked sleepily.

"Morning is coming," Elenna hissed.
"We need to go. Can you direct us to
find Skull Rock?"

The man nodded. "It's half a
morning's walk, on the other side of
the island. Head for the sunrise. But be
careful. Bixara will still be out there."

"Thank you for your help, and for

the shelter," Elenna said, then she and Daltec hurried out into the pale dawn.

They travelled as fast as their weary legs allowed, keeping their faces to the silver disc of the sun, which was rising all too quickly over the horizon.

"We'll never make it in time," Elenna said.

Daltec gazed into his ring as they stumbled on over the rocky heathland.

"Tom's in shackles," Daltec told Elenna. "Hafor and Venga are leading him up a hill. It looks like half the castle are with them." Then he gasped. "They're chaining him up!"

Elenna stopped to look at the vision, panic searing through her. Tom was at the top of a hill, struggling as four of Hafor's warriors fastened him to a huge rock. Outlined clearly against the grey sky, the rock looked rather like a skull, complete with gaping eye sockets and a wide, grinning mouth.

Hafor stormed towards Tom, wielding his jewelled axe.

"We're too late!" Elenna cried, her heart clenching painfully. "I can't watch…" But though she felt sick and dizzy, she couldn't tear her eyes away

from the vision. Tom's arms were spread wide, his chest exposed as Hafor bore down on him. But his eyes were as fierce and defiant as ever.

"Killing me won't save you," Tom told Hafor. "You have to give the Beast her egg back."

"Never!" Hafor cried. Then, instead of raising his axe, he drew something from his cloak.

Tom's belt! Elenna realised.

"I've always wanted a way to speak with my dear friend, Bixara!" Hafor said bitterly. Then he lifted the belt so that Tom's red jewel glinted in the light from the rising sun.

"Bixara!" Hafor shouted. "This is the villain that stole your egg! He has destroyed it, and I bring him to you as an offering to end our conflict. Come! Take your revenge!"

Elenna heard the loud flap of wingbeats. It took a moment to realise the sound wasn't coming from the vision before her, but from the sky. She looked up to see a mighty dragon, its scales shimmering in a kaleidoscope of blues and purples and greens, flying right overhead. She took aim with her bow, but the Beast was already out of range, flying fast towards the sun.

"Can you magic us closer?" Elenna asked Daltec.

The wizard swallowed. "I'll try," he said weakly. "Take my hand." Elenna gripped it tightly. A flash of blue light blinded her, and her stomach lurched. She blinked to find herself standing before the hill from the vision, with Daltec at her side. Tom was at the top of the hill, his head held high, and his gaze defiant as Bixara flapped towards him. Elenna fitted an arrow to her bow. But as she took aim, a plume of searing blue-white flame shot from Bixara's jaws, straight towards Tom.

"No!" The scream tore itself from Elenna's throat as the fire engulfed her friend. She let her arrow fly. It sped through the air, straight and true, driving deep into Bixara's flank. The dragon screeched in fury, then flapped back into the sky, sending another burning jet of fire towards the gathered warriors below. They scattered, crying out in terror and panic. But Elenna's eyes were on Tom's withered corpse,

still hanging from the skull-shaped
rock. There was little left of him now
but bones. Her knees buckled and she
sagged to the ground, bile rising in her
throat and her eyes blurring with tears.

It's all over…Tom's dead…

STORY TWO

BIXARA'S REVENGE

Merival stands alone.

There has been no word of King Hugo, Captain Harkman, nor the boy travelling with them. I wish for their safety, but I fear that my letter has led the three right to their doom. And now, I am afraid, Avantia is without hope.

Who can we rely on now, if not these three? Who can possibly keep Avantia safe from the new villains of the north?

Rutger

CURSED

Elenna raced up the hill at Daltec's side, almost blinded by hot tears as she stumbled over the rugged ground. Suddenly, Daltec gasped.

"He's alive!" he cried, pointing. Elenna wiped her eyes, and saw that although Tom's body was shrivelled beyond recognition, one of his hands was moving. Her heart squeezed painfully, a whimper escaping her lips. *He must be in so much pain!* She broke into a run, and as she came near she saw he wasn't burned at all. He was...old. *Really* old. His clothes hung loose, and sagging, wrinkled skin the colour of parchment clung to his bones. His hair was white and gossamer-thin. Tom's eyes followed her as she approached, his toothless mouth working as if he were trying to speak.

"Tom!" Elenna choked on tears as she gently took hold of his wasted hand. His wrist was so narrow now, it could easily pass through the manacles that held him to the rock. Elenna did this for him, taking care not to tear his translucent skin. Tom lifted his freed hand to his face and felt his features all over with trembling fingers.

"What's happened to me?" he rasped. His eyes flicked between Elenna and Daltec, wide with confusion.

Elenna shook her head, unable to find the words.

"Bixara's fiery breath has aged you," Daltec told Tom. Shouting rang out from the foot of the hill, and Elenna looked down to see Hafor's men returning now Bixara was gone.

"Haven't they done enough already!" Daltec snapped. He conjured a thick grey fog to hide them from view.

"We have to get you out of here," Elenna told Tom. As she slipped his other wrist from the manacles, his knees buckled. Elenna took him in her arms, catching him before he could fall. He felt as light as an infant. She

and Daltec half led, half carried Tom
down the hill under cover of Daltec's
magical fog. They hurried on until the
soldiers' shouts had faded, and the
shadowy trunks of trees loomed in the
mist. Elenna gently lowered Tom on to

a fallen tree stump. He let out a groan as he sank down.

Elenna turned to her friend. He was so thin and bent she was sure that even if Daltec gave him his weapons, he would be too weak to lift them. It seemed unlikely he could even stand unaided. But his eyes, blue and determined: they were his own.

"Can you magic him better?" Elenna asked Daltec. "Or can we use Epos's healing talon?"

The wizard shook his head. "Epos's talon heals injuries, not old age. And I know of no magic that can undo this spell. We need to get Tom back to the palace, and call the Circle of Wizards. Maybe one of them can help." Daltec wouldn't meet her gaze, and from his bowed shoulders, Elenna could see he didn't hold out much hope for Tom.

While there's blood in my veins, I'm not giving up on him! she vowed. Then a sudden thought struck her.

"What about the egg?" she asked. "It made Hafor young. Maybe we can use that to heal Tom?"

Daltec looked up. Elenna saw hope kindle in his eyes, but, at the same moment Tom reached out and gripped her wrist, so hard it almost hurt.

"Don't risk it!" he wheezed. "That's exactly what Hafor will expect you to do. It's more…" Tom stopped, coughing, then went on. "It's more important to save King Hugo. If I die, then so be it. Promise me you'll save the king!" Tom's eyes bored into

Elenna as if reading her heart.

Elenna wanted to tell him the exact opposite – that she would do everything in her power to save *him*. But she knew Tom would never forgive himself if he survived and the king didn't. And His Majesty had a wife and a child to think of – not to mention a kingdom to rule.

"I promise!" she told him.

Satisfied, Tom let his gaze drop. "I… I need to sleep," he said, his head nodding and his eyes falling closed. Daltec wrapped an arm around him to stop him toppling from the log.

"Look after him," Elenna told Daltec. "I'm going to free Hugo and Harkman. Then I'm going to get that egg. Just keep Tom alive!"

2

A RACE AGAINST TIME

Barely aware of her own aching body, Elenna raced across the rocky terrain of Thalassi, heading back towards Hafor's Hall. The sun had risen fully now. Spiders' webs shone in the grass, and the sky was clear and blue, but to Elenna, everything seemed dark and grey. The sound of Tom's laboured breathing played in her mind. *Hang*

on, Tom! But how long could he possibly last? *Hafor will pay for what he has done!* she vowed.

Only when the stark walls of Hafor's Hall were in sight did Elenna stop to think. *I can't just burst in...I need a plan.* She dipped behind a gorse bush and peered up at the fortress's ramparts. All along the walls, fur-clad men with bulging muscles stood beside crossbows and catapults. The fjord before the structure was busy with patrolling longships. But the deep, dark water led almost to the fortress gate. *That's my best hope...*

She hurried from bush to bush towards the water's edge, where thick clumps of rushes hid her from

view. There, she waded into the
water, gasping at its icy touch. As her
chest went under, her body began to
shudder with the shock of the cold,
but Elenna forced herself to take
steady, even breaths. She spotted a
longship making its way towards
the harbour, and ducked her head

beneath the waves. The freezing water clamped about her skull like a vice and she clenched her teeth against the pain. Pushing off from the bank, she swam underwater until she reached the shadow of the longship. Surfacing right by the hull, hidden from above by the curve of its timbers, Elenna clung to the wood, letting the ship carry her with it.

"Hafor really has lost it now," a male voice said close above her. Realising it came from the boat, Elenna held her breath, listening.

"Tell me about it," another voice said. "To lock up the king of all Avantia, you'd have to be mad. But there's not much we can do. Not with Bixara on the loose…"

"You're right there," the first voice said. "I'd rather deal with a mad king than her fire any day." The longship drew level with the jetty and slid to a halt. Elenna kept low in the water, hiding in the shadows while the men clattered about, mooring the ship and disembarking.

Once their booted feet had stomped away, she took a deep breath and dipped back below the surface. She re-emerged right beneath the deserted jetty's slatted planks, where strips of daylight dappled the water. Peering towards the rocky shore, she could just make out the men from the ship disappearing through the fortress gates. *This is my chance!* Before the doors could swing closed, Elenna heaved herself from the icy water and on to the jetty. Her hands and feet were clumsy and numb, but she couldn't wait to warm up. She glanced right and left, then ducked low and ran.

The cloak of the last of the soldiers swept through the doors as Elenna reached them. She darted silently after the warriors, slipped behind a wooden pillar and waited until they had filed into the banqueting hall.

Thinking back to Daltec's vision, Elenna tried to get her bearings. *Which way to the dungeon?* she wondered. The corridor where Tom and the others had been housed was presumably the living quarters. It seemed unlikely the dungeons would be there, so she ducked down the other corridor instead. Fitting an arrow to her bow, she crept onwards, hugging the wall and stopping to listen at each door she passed. One stood open a crack. A clattering sound came from inside. Elenna peered through the narrow gap and saw Venga fastening her leg armour with leather straps.

Lifting her bow, Elenna slammed the door open and leapt through. "Don't make a sound!" she hissed, aiming the tip of her arrow at Venga's chest.

Wide-eyed with alarm, Venga raised her hands. Up close, Elenna could see dark circles beneath the woman's eyes, and deep worry lines on her brow.

Venga sighed. "I'm guessing you're here to rescue King Hugo?" she said.

Elenna nodded. "You must know that

what your father's doing is wrong,"
she said. "He's left my best friend
close to death and jailed the king of
Avantia. Meanwhile, your own people
are almost starving. This can't go on."

Venga sighed again and looked at

her feet. "I think Father's sick," she said. "Since he got his hands on that egg, all he can think about is staying young. It's poisoned him. Everyone's scared to cross him. And now he can actually talk with the Beast, things can only get worse. Still, what can I do? I've tried talking to him, but he just gets angry."

Elenna clenched her jaw. "Well, you need to do *something*. For the sake of everyone on this island. You can start with freeing King Hugo. Take me to the dungeon." Elenna stepped closer to the woman, her arrow almost touching Venga's chest. "And no tricks."

"No tricks," Venga agreed. "Come." The woman peered out through her chamber door, checking both ways, then ducked out. With the

tip of her arrow brushing Venga's back,
Elenna followed, soon reaching the
far end of the corridor. Venga grabbed
a flaming torch from a bracket on
the wall and led Elenna through a
door, down a narrow stone staircase.
At the bottom there was another
corridor, this one dug into the ground
itself. They hurried past heavy-looking
doors and soon reached a dungeon
at the end, barred with rusted iron.
Elenna could hear a scuffling within,
then saw Harkman and Hugo peering
through the bars as Venga approached.

"We're here to free you," Elenna
whispered, "but we must be quiet."

"Elenna," Hugo said hoarsely, his
eyes filling with tears as he spoke. "I'm
so sorry. If there was any way I could

have saved Tom…" His voice trailed off. Venga unlocked the cell and it opened with an echoing *creak*.

"Tom's not dead," Elenna said.

"Thank goodness!" Harkman cried, then clapped a hand over his mouth. "I'm so glad to hear that!" he added more softly.

"But he is very sick," Elenna told them. "He's been stricken by a curse. As soon as you two are safe, I'm going to help him."

"I think not!" Hafor's furious voice bellowed from behind them. Elenna spun to see the now youthful Thalassian king charge down the stone staircase with four armed warriors behind him. "Lock them up!" he ordered his men.

1

3

OUTNUMBERED

Elenna raised her bow and took
aim as the huge warriors marched
towards her, but in the close confines
of the tunnel, the bow's tip caught
the ceiling, knocking her aim off. A
barrel-chested man with an eyepatch
lunged to snatch the bow from her
grip. Another warrior tried to catch
her arm, but Elenna drove her fist
smartly into his nose, breaking it with

a sickening *crack*.

Captain Harkman and King Hugo leapt from their cell, fists raised. Venga snatched a long knife from her belt and handed it to Elenna, then drew her own sword. But at that moment, at least a dozen more soldiers clattered down the stairs into the corridor.

"You're outnumbered!" Hafor cried. "Drop your weapons!"

"Never!" Elenna growled. But the soldier with her bow aimed it at Hugo's throat.

"Drop them, or your king dies!" Hafor repeated, his teeth bared like a rabid dog. With the whole corridor full of armed soldiers, Elenna had no choice. She let her knife fall to the floor with a clatter.

Hafor turned to the guard whose nose Elenna had broken. "Tie her up!" he snapped, jabbing the tip of his sword towards Elenna. "My daughter,

too. Venga will pay for her treachery!"

"My pleasure!" the man spat though the blood streaming down his face. Elenna backed away from him, but her foot came up against the dungeon wall and he grabbed her shoulder roughly. "Stay still, you little hellcat!" he growled, taking a length of rope from his cloak, wrapping it about her ankles and hefting her upside down. Another guard gripped Venga's shoulders, while Harkman and Hugo were shoved back into their cell.

"Now! Tell me where that brat of a boy is," Hafor demanded.

"He's dead!" Elenna cried. And as she said the words her heart clenched. *He really could be…*

"Ha!" Hafor grinned broadly and

turning towards the king. "Hugo – I always thought you were weak. Fancy making a mere *boy* Master of the Beasts. Ridiculous! No wonder you've ended up shut in a dungeon. How is a child supposed to dominate a Beast?"

Elenna could feel all the blood thumping in her head, from fury as well as being suspended upside down. "Tom has never dominated anyone!" she said. "He always used his powers for Good."

"Well, maybe that's where he went wrong," Hafor said. "Now I've got his magic jewels, I plan to make Bixara do my bidding!" Hafor tapped his waist, and Elenna saw he wore Tom's belt. The red jewel glowed softly in the gloom. The sight gave Elenna an idea. *Maybe Bixara can hear Hafor through the jewel? Well, if she can, it's about time she found out the truth from Hafor's own lips...*

"Stealing a Beast's egg to keep yourself young runs against all the laws of nature," Elenna said. "No one lives for ever, Hafor... You will pay sorely in the end."

"I decide what is right!" Hafor growled. "The egg is *mine* and I will use it as *I* see fit! I can live for ever if I wish!" He stepped towards Elenna, bending down low to grip her hair. With Hafor's face right before her, Elenna could clearly see new lines around his eyes and mouth and grey streaks in his curled hair. She could smell the meaty stink of his breath.

"Tell me where the wizard boy is," Hafor snarled.

"Never!" Elenna said.

Hafor sighed. "Do I have to remind you, your own arrow is pointed at your king? How will you feel when he dies with it buried in his heart?"

"Don't tell him anything, Elenna," Hugo said from behind her, and she felt proud to hear no trace of a waver in the king's stern voice.

Suddenly, the high, bloodcurdling screech of a dragon echoed from somewhere above them. Hafor's eyes, so close to Elenna's, widened in panic as the tunnel shook, dirt and chips of stone falling to the floor.

Despite the pain of the blood thundering in her skull, Elenna

smiled. "The Beast is coming," she
said, softly. "I think you had better
run."

Hafor growled like a caged animal,
right in Elenna's ear. With a final tug,
he let her hair go. "Guards! Lock

up these traitors. I have something I must do." As Hafor turned and hurried away, his troops parting before him, the tunnel juddered once more. Another screech, closer this time, rang out above. Elenna recognised in its tone the anguished, furious scream of a mother who has lost her child.

Bixara!

BIXARA'S RAGE

Elenna's vision was blurred from being upside down for so long, but she could see the passage was packed from wall to wall with armoured guards, all wielding axes and swords. Some looked fearful, glancing upwards as Bixara's wild screech echoed towards them. But many scowled with fury. Suddenly, the tunnel rocked so fiercely that even the big man holding Elenna staggered.

Venga, still in the grip of a broad-chested solider, caught Elenna's eye, and winked. Then, before the juddering stopped, the woman kicked out, shoving a nearby guard in the small of the back. The blow catapulted him towards Elenna. Using the momentum of her kick, Venga slammed her head back into the face of the guard that held her. Elenna bent at the waist, lifting herself up to grab a knife from the belt of the guard Venga had kicked. She swiped upwards, slicing through the rope binding her feet. Gripping the collar of her broken-nosed captor, she righted herself, then thrust him hard away from her and sank into a crouch, wielding her stolen blade.

Venga had snatched a knife from her boot and brandished it too, her eyes flashing like fire. "I don't want to fight my own people," she said. "But I will if I must. The roof's going to come down any moment. Bixara is here! I offer you the chance to flee while you still can!" A huge *crash* rang out above, and the floor leapt. A crack as wide as Elenna's fist opened in the ceiling and more dust and stones rained down. The soldiers exchanged terrified looks, then turned and ran.

Venga threw open the door to Harkman and Hugo's cell. "Follow me!" she told them. "I know a secret way out." She led Elenna, Hugo and

Harkman back along the shuddering corridor, stopping by one of the heavy doors about halfway along. She unlocked it, and hurried through. The door led into a dark, upwards-sloping tunnel that smelled of rotten seaweed and fish. Water dripped down the walls, and at the end of the tunnel, daylight streamed down what looked like a ramp, hewn from stone.

"Up here," Venga said. The daylight brightened as Elenna followed Venga towards the ramp, Hugo and Harkman right behind her. They emerged outside the fortress walls beside a small rowing boat docked in a deep stone channel leading back to the fjord.

Venga held the boat steady while

Hugo, Harkman and Elenna all stepped in.

"I must go back," Venga told them. "I have to try to get my father to see sense."

Elenna put her hand on the woman's shoulder, and squeezed.

"Good luck," she said, "and thank you."

Venga nodded. Then she pushed the boat away from the slipway, and set off back towards the fortress. Elenna rowed with all her strength, driving the boat quickly along its narrow channel and out on to the sunlit fjord, emerging right in front of Hafor's keep. Her belly tightened with dread at the sight that greeted them.

Bixara's huge, shimmering form swooped over the battlements, breathing icy blue fire at the soldiers manning the catapults. Crashes and booms rang out as rocks missed their target and clattered down, hitting the jetty and harbour. Part of the fortress roof and a length of the ramparts had been smashed. Men were running backwards and forwards, and Elenna saw others who hobbled like old men, their hair turned grey and their muscles wasted away.

"We should stay and help!" Hugo said, staring in concern.

"No, sire," Harkman said. "There is nothing we can do against that Beast. It's Hafor's problem, and he can solve it. I have to get you to safety."

"Get back to the mainland," Elenna said. "If we are lucky, Rutger will already have sent for help from the palace. I'll meet you in Merival as soon as I can."

Harkman frowned. "Why? Where are you going?" he asked.

"I have to get Bixara's egg. It's Tom's only hope." Before Harkman or Hugo could say anything, Elenna turned and leapt from the boat back into the icy fjord, and swam towards the chaotic scenes on shore.

She dragged herself, cold and dripping, from the water and up on to the rocky harbour beside what remained of the jetty. As Elenna stood, Venga re-emerged from the keep, her face draining of colour as she took in the destruction all around her. As she flew low, Bixara's huge blue eye came to rest on Venga. The Beast let out a hiss of rage and swooped straight towards her.

"Venga! Run!" Elenna cried.

Venga glanced back just in time to see Bixara dive. The woman broke into a sprint, racing towards the

remains of a watchtower, but her foot
caught on a fallen beam and she fell,
sprawling headlong on the ground.

Elenna was already running.
She reached Venga just as Bixara
landed. The Beast towered above

them, her scales all the colours of the ocean. With her glittering wings and righteous fury, she was beautiful and terrible all at once. Her massive jaws opened, ready to breathe her deadly fire. Scanning the ground, Elenna spotted a discarded spear. She snatched it up and lunged, aiming for Bixara's muscled thigh.

The tip of the spear bit deep, driving between two scales. Bixara lifted her head and roared, wrenching her leg free. Her head writhed from side to side in pain as she flapped her wings and rose back into the sky. Venga scrambled up and raced for the shelter of the nearby watchtower.

Elenna was about to follow, but glancing up, she saw Bixara's furious eyes narrow, her jaws opening to send a blazing jet of fire straight towards her. Elenna threw herself down into a sideways roll, diving under a boat's upturned hull. Flames sizzled and spat all around her small shelter. She pulled her arms and legs closer, lest any stray sparks should touch her skin. The onslaught seemed to go on for ever, but finally Bixara's deadly blast stopped and all was quiet. Without waiting for the Beast to draw another breath, Elenna dived out from under the boat and ran for the fortress. Expecting at any moment to feel the touch of deadly fire, she didn't dare glance back. She pushed on at top speed, leapt through the heavy doors, and slammed them shut.

5

HOPE SHATTERED

Inside the antechamber, broken beams
littered the floor, and guards were
slumped against the walls. Elenna's
skin tightened as she noticed the
soldiers' flesh was wizened like old
apples, their hair grey and thin. One
reached a gnarled hand towards
her, wheezing for help. But Elenna
couldn't stop. She took the stairs

two at a time and burst into the banqueting hall.

The ceiling was partly caved in, the tables lying smashed beneath heavy beams. Upturned chairs and broken crockery were scattered on the floor. But the room was empty. With crashes and booms from outside ringing in her ears, Elenna hurried towards the tapestry at the back of the room. As she set foot on the royal dais, the tapestry twitched aside. Hafor emerged, carrying Bixara's egg, half wrapped in a velvet cloth.

The Thalassian's youth had been fully restored again. His hair gleamed and his muscles bulged beneath his leathers. As his blue eyes locked with Elenna's, he scowled.

"Get out!" he hissed. "You have no right to be here. The egg is mine!" He cradled it in his arms, jealously.

Disgust churned Elenna's stomach.

She shook her head. "The egg isn't yours, Hafor," she said. "It's Bixara's. You have to give it back. She won't stop killing people until you do."

"I will never give it back!" Hafor growled, tugging a knife from his belt while cradling the egg in his free arm.

Elenna gathered her strength and threw herself towards Hafor. He stabbed out with his knife, but she grabbed his wrist in both hands and twisted it up behind his back, forcing him to double over and drop the weapon. Struggling to free himself from her grip, Hafor lost his hold on the egg...

No! Elenna's heart skipped.

Almost as if time had slowed, she watched the precious egg hit the ground and shatter. Hafor wrenched himself from her grip as she stared in horror at the broken egg, still half shrouded in its velvet wrap.

"Look what you've done, you stupid girl!" Hafor cried. Beneath the blanket, something twitched. With another jerking movement, a small, pearly-white head appeared, peeking from the velvet folds. Elenna gasped as the wide, round eyes of a baby dragon gazed back up at her.

"Out of my way!" Hafor screamed, slamming his full weight into her shoulder, shoving her sideways. Elenna's boot caught the edge of the dais, and she toppled off it, hitting the ground hard and cracking the side of her head. Shaking the dizziness away, she looked up to see Hafor scoop the hatchling into his arms and race past her from the hall, leaving a pile of pearly blue eggshell fragments in his wake.

Sickness rolling over her in waves, Elenna staggered up and lifted one of the shiny shards of shell. A burning tear trickled down her cheek. *The egg was Tom's only hope. And I broke it.*

A shadow fell over her suddenly, as something large blocked the light from one of the narrow windows. She looked up to see a swirling blue-green eye staring in at her.

Bixara!

The Beast's eye swivelled down to the mess of broken shell, then turned back to look at Elenna again. Bixara's slitted pupil narrowed.

"It's...n-not what it seems," Elenna stammered, lifting her hands. "Your baby's alive. Hafor has taken it!" But the eye had already withdrawn, and, with a thunderous crash, Bixara's jaws snapped closed around the window frame. The dragon wrenched her head from side to side, tearing a huge chunk of wall free. Beams crashed down from the ceiling. A massive section of roof collapsed, blocking the door. Dust filled the air.

Looking for an escape, Elenna noticed that the huge tapestry at the back of the room had come away from its fastenings and slumped to the ground. She raced towards it and hefted it up, just as Bixara thrust her

huge snout back into the hall. Terror
giving her strength, Elenna tugged
the vast piece of fabric towards
the dragon and heaved it over her
jaws. Then she turned and ran.

Through a hole smashed in one
wall, Elenna glimpsed a narrow

stair. *The battlements!* She scrambled
upwards, quickly emerging on
to the roof. A narrow walkway
led from the battlements to the
roof of a watchtower that looked
largely intact. Glancing down at
the wreckage of the harbour below,

Elenna made a run for it. But, before she'd even got halfway, she heard a furious screech. Looking back, she saw Bixara rise on shimmering wings, lifting a clawed foot and slamming it down on the end of the walkway. The bridge leapt beneath Elenna's feet, then dropped away. Her stomach flipped. She scrabbled around for a handhold as she fell, but found nothing to grip... The hard rock of the harbour sped up to meet her. Elenna tucked into a roll and threw out her arms to break her fall.

"Ooof!" Pain exploded in her shoulders and back as she landed. Almost at once, in a torrent of wingbeats, Bixara alighted beside her. The dragon's massive, shining form filled Elenna's view. Winded and dazed, she tried to move, but every part of her hurt and her limbs were too heavy to lift. Bixara glared down at Elenna, her swirling eyes filled with hate. The dragon opened her mighty jaws. Elenna closed her eyes, waiting for the deadly fire to strike. Her final thoughts turned to Tom. Her friend.

I wonder if he'll be waiting for me on the other side...

1

HAFOR'S LAST STAND

"Elenna!" Tom's voice rasped weakly from nearby. Elenna's heart gave a strange, startled leap. *Am I dead?*

She opened her eyes to see Bixara still looming over her. But between her and the dragon, partly blocking her view, stood the thin and wizened figure of an old man. He held a shield aloft. Blue flames of dragon fire licked around the edges of the wood.

Tom! He's alive… And so am I.

But Tom's limbs were shaking.
His bowed back sank lower as he
withstood the onslaught of Bixara's
fiery breath. Elenna shot to her feet,

her courage restored at the sight
of her friend, and leapt to his side.
Putting her hand next to Tom's, she
held the shield steady. Bixara's flames
blasted against the wood, but Elenna
planted her feet wide and braced
her muscles. She couldn't let the fire
strike Tom.

Finally, the sizzling jet stopped.

Elenna and Tom stood side by side,
panting, gingerly peering up over the
top of the shield. The Beast glared
back at them, her nostrils flared and
her eyes blazing with anger and hurt.

"We're not your enemy!" Elenna
shouted. But without Tom's red
jewel, there was no way to make the
Beast understand. Bixara lifted a
clawed foot and swiped for Elenna,

cannoning her sideways into Tom. As light as a child and with no strength to save himself, Tom shot through the air, landing in the fjord with barely a splash.

"NO!" Elenna screamed as she leapt to her feet, still clutching Tom's shield. Her gaze flicked between Bixara, ready to swipe again, and Tom's body, floating in the icy water. But at that moment, the Beast's head came up, her eyes fixing on something beyond Elenna. She spread her massive wings and took flight.

"Tom!" Elenna cried, rushing towards the fjord. She bent her knees, ready to leap in after him, but a familiar rowing boat floated into view. *King Hugo and*

Captain Harkman! They drew up alongside Tom and leaned over to pull him aboard.

"Elenna, look!" Daltec's voice shouted from nearby. Elenna glanced over to see the young wizard holding off a pair of guards with a crackling stream of magical energy. With his other hand, he pointed up at the ramparts of the fort. Turning, Elenna spotted what Daltec and Bixara had both seen. *Hafor!* He was standing high on the half-gutted roof of his hall, holding Bixara's struggling baby in his arms. Hovering above him, the great dragon let out an anguished shriek.

"Back off, or I'll drop this useless runt!" Hafor roared up at Bixara. The

pale baby Beast squirmed and
let out a puff of white smoke. Its
shiny eyes were round with terror.
Bixara screeched again, but didn't
dive. Spotting a fallen bow among
the wreckage that surrounded her,
Elenna snatched it up, took an arrow
from her quiver and aimed at Hafor.
But looking between the crazed man
and the frantic Beast hovering above
him, Elenna hesitated. *If I kill Hafor,
the baby will fall!*

"If you can hit Hafor, do it!" Daltec
called. Elenna glanced at him to see
the soldiers he had been fighting were
both staring at Hafor, too.

"But – the baby!" she called back.
Daltec smiled and lifted a hand,
which was glowing with silvery

energy. "Remember the apples," he called.

Elenna understood at once. She turned back to Hafor. He was ageing rapidly now, his curled hair iron grey, his scowling face deeply lined. Elenna let her arrow fly. It whizzed through the air and sliced cleanly through Hafor's shoulder, lodging there. With a howl of pain, Hafor dropped the baby dragon, then ducked out of sight.

Daltec, standing ready, hurled a shining bubble of silver energy towards the plummeting hatchling. The gleaming orb rose to envelop the baby, slowing its fall. Elenna watched as the bubble drifted lower, losing brightness as it fell.

Venga strode forwards and put her
hands out just in time to snatch it
from the air as Daltec's magic bubble
popped, leaving her cradling a small,
shaking dragon to her chest.

Bixara swooped and landed before

Venga. The dragon's eyes swam with shimmering blues and greens as she took in the sight of her baby. Venga bowed her head, and set the small creature on the ground. With a shake of its pearlescent wings, the little dragon hopped over to its mother, leapt up on to her leg, and clung on tight.

An awed silence had fallen, but it was suddenly broken by Captain Harkman's panicked cry. "Tom!"

Elenna looked over to see that Harkman and Hugo had reached the jetty. The captain was holding Tom's frail body in his arms, his face etched with horror and grief.

"He has no pulse!" Harkman cried.

7

JUST DESERTS

Elenna watched, cold and empty
inside, as Harkman laid Tom's lifeless
body on the jetty. Hugo solemnly
bowed his head.

No...no... He can't be gone! As
Elenna stepped closer to Tom's still
form, the sounds around her seemed
muffled and distant, as if she was
trapped in a terrible dream. But
before she could reach her friend,

Bixara flapped into her path, her huge head cocked and her gleaming eyes on Tom.

"Leave him alone!" Elenna shouted. Hugo backed away from the dragon, waving his arms as if to fend the Beast off, but Bixara snatched Tom up in her mighty jaws and surged away.

Elenna stared at the empty space where Tom had been. A picture flashed through her mind. The field of animal skeletons she and Daltec had passed through, all picked clean. *Is she going to eat him? Or feed him to her baby?* Elenna found she was shaking all over.

"Kill the girl!" a cracked old voice screamed, breaking the silence that had fallen. Elenna turned to see Hafor stride from his fort, her arrow still jutting from his shoulder. He looked older than before, his face and hands covered in dark blotches. Nobody moved. "Do it now!" Hafor

yelled, searching out the eyes of his guards. Still they didn't obey.

"Father, your time is over," Venga said, stepping softly towards him. "You must stop this folly."

"Never!" Hafor cried. "I will live for ever!" But even as he said the words, Elenna could see his body shrinking before her eyes, the muscles shrivelling away. His hair began falling out in white clumps. "No!" he screamed, his voice weak and reedy as he put a hand to his bald scalp, and then to the red jewel in Tom's belt.

"Bixara! If you make me young again, I will do your bidding. We can rule together!" Hafor searched the sky, but there was no sign of the Beast. His back bowed lower and his fingers curled to crooked claws. He tried to speak again, but his voice was too weak for Elenna to hear. She watched, unable to turn away as his lined skin crumpled like the peel of a rotting fruit. His whole body seemed to cave in on itself. Soon, barely more than a hunched skeleton remained, a grimacing skull. His thin lips mouthed another silent "No," before he sank to his knees and fell forwards. His cloak floated to the ground, flat and empty.

Hafor was gone.

Venga stood trembling, staring at the cloak. Elenna tuned away from it, her heart aching for Tom. Hafor's death wouldn't bring him back...

"Elenna, look!" Daltec suddenly

cried. He showed the ring on his hand. Blinking back tears, Elenna crossed the rubble-strewn ground towards the wizard, and stared down at the red-tinged vision. She saw a huge nest, constructed of tree branches and lined with bushes and ferns.

Inside the nest sat a gleaming blue-white egg. And beside the egg lay Tom. But not the wizened ancient skeleton he had become. Tom the boy! The vision enlarged, showing a craggy peak, and Bixara standing over her nest with her baby at her side. The Beast opened her wings wide, lifted her head, and let out a triumphant screech.

Elenna found herself grinning and crying at the same time, big

wrenching sobs with tears pouring
down her cheeks. "She saved
him! The Beast saved Tom!"

Later, outside the inn back in Merival, Tom and Elenna watched as Venga and Rutger shook hands, watched by King Hugo, Captain Harkman and Daltec.

"I promise you, Thalassi will never raid Merival again," Venga told Rutger. "In fact, I plan to open trade routes with the mainland, and start a breeding programme to restock our fields with herds. I hope soon I'll be able to replace all Merival's livestock. It's the least my people can do." Venga turned to Elenna.

"I want to give you this as a token of my thanks for freeing us from Bixara's wrath," she said, holding out

Hafor's jewel-encrusted axe.

"Thank you," Elenna said.

"I want to thank you too," Tom told Elenna. "You saved my life."

Elenna smiled. It was so good to see him back to his old – or rather, *young* – self. "You saved mine too," Elenna replied. "Although, what Daltec was thinking bringing you into the middle of a battle in that state, I don't know!" Elenna shot Daltec a mock-angry frown.

Daltec looked sheepish. "Tom is very persuasive when he decides he has something to do, as well you know," the wizard said.

"Well, I can't argue with that," Elenna said. She turned back to Tom. "Maybe you'll take this as a warning

that you need to rest once in a while?"
she said.

Tom shrugged. "Seeing how well
you've all handled everything without
me, I was thinking I should retire…"

Elenna gaped at him in shock, then
noticed the twinkle in his eyes. "As

if!" she said, grinning.

Tom grinned back. "You're right," he said. "I'm not ready to pass on my sword and shield yet. We definitely work best as a team!"

THE END

READ ALL THE BOOKS IN SERIES 26:
THE FOUR MASTERS!

TEKNOS
THE OCEAN CRAWLER

MALLIX
THE SILENT STALKER

SILEXA
THE STONE CAT

KYRON
LORD OF FIRE

CONGRATULATIONS,
YOU HAVE COMPLETED
THIS QUEST!

At the end of each chapter you were
awarded a special gold coin.
The QUEST in this book was
worth an amazing 14 coins.

Look at the Beast Quest totem picture
overleaf to see how far you've come
in your journey to become

MASTER OF THE BEASTS.

The more books you read,
the more coins you will collect!

Do you want your own
Beast Quest Totem?
1. Cut out and collect the coin below
2. Go to the Beast Quest website
3. Download and print out your totem
4. Add your coin to the totem

www.beastquest.co.uk

31901067043200

550+ COINS
MASTER OF THE BEASTS

410 COINS
HERO

350 COINS
WARRIOR

230 COINS
KNIGHT

180 COINS
SQUIRE

44 COINS
PAGE

8 COINS
APPRENTICE

550+
515
480
445
410
395
380
365
350
320
290
260
230
217
206
191
180
146
112
78
44
30
19
8